The Queen Cat

YEARLING BOOKS/YOUNG YEARLINGS/YEARLING CLASSICS are designed especially to entertain and enlighten young people. Patricia Reilly Giff, consultant to this series, received her bachelor's degree from Marymount College and a master's degree in history from St. John's University. She holds a Professional Diploma in Reading and a Doctorate of Humane Letters from Hofstra University. She was a teacher and reading consultant for many years, and is the author of numerous books for young readers.

THE
QUEEN
CAT

Ann Turnbull

Illustrated by Jan Lewis

A Young Yearling Book

Published by
Dell Publishing
a division of
Bantam Doubleday Dell Publishing Group, Inc.
666 Fifth Avenue
New York, New York 10103

This work was first published in Great Britain in 1989 by
Macdonald Children's Books.

ISBN: 0-440-40511-4

Reprinted by arrangement with Simon & Schuster
Young Books

Printed in the United States of America

March 1992

10 9 8 7 6 5 4 3 2 1

WES

For Julie

Chapter One

"Wake up, Mew-sheri, wake up! You must put ashes on your face and tangles in your hair."

Mew-sheri struggled with sleep. What was Zaita saying? Ashes? Tangles? Usually her sisters nagged her to *wash* her face and *comb* her hair.

"Wake up!" persisted Zaita.

In the distance Mew-sheri heard a high continuous sound: the sound of women wailing for the dead.

She sat up, wide awake.

Zaita's face was smeared with ashes and her black eyeliner had run.

"The Queen Cat is dead," said Zaita.

"The Queen Cat?"

All Mew-sheri's life the Queen Cat had lived in the temple of Bastet, the temple of the Cat Goddess, in the heart of the city of Bubastis.

Mew-sheri had never seen her, but she knew about her because her two sisters were priestesses there. Bastet herself was a gilded statue hidden in a dark sanctuary in the temple. The Queen Cat was her living spirit. When the Queen Cat died the whole city went into mourning.

Mew-sheri got out of bed. Tiya came in, carrying a dish of ash mixed with water, and began smearing Mew-sheri's face.

7

"I can do it!"
said Mew-sheri.
"Let me!"

But Tiya insisted
on doing it for her,
while Zaita untidied her hair.

Tiya and Zaita never let Mew-sheri do anything for herself. Their mother was dead, and because Mew-sheri was much younger than them, they had always looked after her. They bossed her and bothered her. Their father was no better: to him she would always be his baby, the one he nicknamed Mew-sheri, "Pussycat."

Mew-sheri knew that she had a real name: it was Neferet. But no one ever called her that, and it seemed strange and unusable, like a special dress folded away in a cedarwood chest.

When her sisters had finished with her, Mew-sheri looked in the polished bronze mirror. She saw a dirty, ash-streaked face. Her hair, which usually swung on her shoulders like a black bell, stuck out in tangles.

Mew-sheri grinned, then remembered the poor dead cat, and tried to look sad.

"Will there be a new Queen Cat?" she asked.

"Yes," said Tiya. "But she will not be one of the temple cats; she will come from outside."

"Who will choose her?"

"She will not be chosen," Tiya said. "She will come. She may come of her own free will, or she may be brought to the temple by someone who has found her and recognized the goddess in her. Anyone might find her, even a child."

"A child?"

Tiya smiled. "Yes.
Perhaps even you,
Pussycat."

"How would I know
her—if I found her?"
asked Mew-sheri. "What color will she
be? Will she be big? Will she be
beautiful?"

"She won't be any particular color or
size, and she may not even be beautiful,"
said Tiya. "But she will be special, and if
you found her—you would simply know.
You would know that she was the one."

11

Mew-sheri was staring at her sister with big eyes. "I'm going to find her," she said.

Zaita was scornful. "Don't be silly. There are thousands of cats in Egypt. She might be any cat, from here in the Delta right down to Nubia."

"But wherever she is now," said Mew-sheri, "she will come to Bubastis, because she is the goddess. And I shall find her."

She went to the window and looked out. Tah-hotep, their father, was a goldsmith in charge of the temple workshop, and their house was near the canal that circled the temple. Mew-sheri could see a cat sitting on the temple wall, washing itself.

It's not you, she thought; you are one of the sacred cats, but you are not the one special cat who will be the new queen.

Below her the street door opened, and
Ahmes, their housekeeper, stepped out,
followed by a maid carrying a large
basket. They were going to market.

"Ahmes!" called Mew-sheri. "Wait for
me! I want to come."

She pattered barefoot down the stairs
and out into the hot street.

"I'm looking for the new Queen Cat,"
she said.

Cats were everywhere: sitting in doorways, looking out through latticed windows, threading hopefully amongst the legs and towropes on the quay, miaowing for scraps in the fish market. Mew-sheri looked at them all, but not one of them seemed to say, "Here I am: the cat you are searching for."

Days and weeks went by, and Mew-sheri had still not found the one special cat. Perhaps, she thought, the cat hasn't arrived in Bubastis yet; perhaps she is in another city, waiting to be recognized.

15

Then Zaita came from the temple with news that Mew-sheri could become a priestess. She was to start in one month's time, on the same day that the new Queen Cat was expected to appear.

Mew-sheri knew that she would serve in the temple for one month in every four like her sisters. She felt happy and scared.

"What will I have to do?" she asked.

"You will walk in the processions," said Tiya, "and sing, and make music."

"And you will help care for the sacred cats," said Zaita.

16

Tah-hotep said, "Pussycat, if you are old enough to be a priestess, it's time you saw something of the world. I have to take the boat upriver to Memphis for a few days on temple business. Do you want to come with me?"

"Oh, yes!" said Mew-sheri. She couldn't wait to go. Surely in a great city like Memphis she would find the new Queen Cat.

Chapter Two

Mew-sheri was disappointed. For a day and a half she had followed her father and his servant Osar around Memphis, visiting temples and markets and houses, and everywhere she went there were cats —ordinary, homely cats.

They're just pussycats, like me, thought Mew-sheri despondently. And now it's time to go home, and I'm still no nearer finding the Queen Cat.

"Are you ready, Pussycat?" her father asked.

"Don't call me that," said Mew-sheri.

It was almost noon. There wasn't time to reach home that day.

"There's an inn on the way back," said Tah-hotep, "just this side of the first fork in the river. We'll spend the night there and go home tomorrow."

They reached the inn in the late afternoon. Mew-sheri saw that the green strip bordering the Nile was narrow and the desert crept close. They tied up the boat and walked inland, past irrigation ditches and fields of flax and barley. It was harvesttime and the people sang as they swung their scythes.

The innkeeper told Tah-hotep they could have the choice of a room inside or they could sleep on the roof. Tah-hotep chose the roof. It was cooler up there during the hot season.

They climbed up the outside steps.

"I want this one!"

Mew-sheri chose a bed on the eastern side of the house. When she looked over the wall next to the bed she saw below rough ground with a cluster of outbuildings—cowsheds and a threshing room. The shadows of the buildings were black on the pale baked earth. Beyond them was the Eastern Desert.

Mew-sheri had never been so close to

the desert before. At first, as she stared at it, it seemed empty and bare, a golden expanse of nothing, shimmering in the heat. Then she began to notice shadows and rocky ridges, crisscrossing tracks, the scar of an old quarry, and some buildings where the quarry workers had probably once lived. A hawk hung in the sky above the quarry, looking for animals among the rocks.

Mew-sheri turned away to the familiar

sight of water and fields. A smell of cooking rose from below.

"Come and eat," said Tah-hotep.

It was after sunset when Mew-sheri went back to the roof. The desert's gold had faded to gray and she could not see the quarry anymore.

She got into bed. She was tired and fell asleep quickly, in spite of the heat.

She awoke suddenly late at night, and did not know why, unless it was the moon shining on her face. She raised herself on her elbows and looked around the rooftop. It was lit by moonlight, and she could see the humped shape of her father in his bed and hear the rhythm of his breathing. She lay down again and tried to sleep, but she was wide awake and fidgety. She got out of bed and pulled on her dress. The roof was still warm from the day's sun, but the night air was cool.

She leaned on the wall and gazed out at the desert.

Something moving in the yard caught her eye. An animal. A cat!

The cat came out of the shadows and sat down in the square of moonlight. It looked up at her, the moon filling its eyes.

It was a big cat, but
slim, with a narrow
face and upright ears,
and as its eyes looked
into hers Mew-sheri
felt her heart begin to
beat fast. She knew,
without a doubt, that
this was the one: the
one special cat who
was the living spirit of
the goddess.

Chapter Three

As Mew-sheri stared, the cat stood up.

Mew-sheri was panic-stricken. She gripped the wall. "Oh, don't go! Please!"

But the cat turned away and began trotting towards the desert.

Mew-sheri did not stop to think. She picked up a linen wrap from the bed and flung it around her shoulders.

She ran down the stairs and out into
the yard. The cat was still in sight,
padding purposefully into the desert.
Mew-sheri ran after her.

The desert, which had looked so smooth
from the roof, felt hard to her bare feet.
The layer of loose sand was thin, and
there were sharp stones poking through.
She picked her way carefully.

The cat was moving ahead fast;
somehow she had to make her stop.

"Puss!" she called. "Please wait!" And, when that failed, "Goddess! Lady! Don't you know your place is in the temple?"

The cat looked around. Her eyes gleamed. Mew-sheri approached cautiously, crouching and putting out a hand. "You must come with me," she pleaded.

But the cat drew back from her touch, turned, and went on moving eastwards. And Mew-sheri, desperate not to lose her, followed.

She looked ahead and saw the barren desert, the far-off quarry, and the relentlessly trotting cat. She looked back and saw the village dwindling in the distance. She longed for the safety of her bed, her father, the walls of the houses.

If only she had not come alone. If only she had woken her father. But it was too late now.

They were still moving on, deeper and deeper into the desert. The cat seemed to know exactly where she was going. Once or twice she looked back, as if to check that Mew-sheri was following.

They came to a track. The cat turned onto it. Mew-sheri saw that it led towards the quarry.

She felt a flutter of fear. Was that where the cat was going? To the old quarry? Mew-sheri didn't want to go there, not to that wild place with the deserted houses nearby. She thought of lions and snakes and the spirits of the dead. But still the cat trotted on.

They were approaching the quarry now. The white scar of the workings shone in the moonlight. Not far away were the empty houses, and it was to them that the track led.

The nearest house had a central doorway and two windows, one on either side. It looked like a face: blind eyes and shouting mouth.

The cat went in through the door and Mew-sheri stood still, rigid with fear.

I can't go in there, she thought. Stories of ghosts and spirits filled her mind.

"Lady, please come out," she called.

But the cat did not come out. Mew-sheri called again. Silence. The cold desert night made her shiver. She felt utterly alone. At last, afraid of losing  the cat, she gathered up all her courage and went in through the dark doorway.

She saw rubble on the floor, a broken roof, moonlight shining in and catching the eyes of the cat. No ghosts. No spirits. The banging of her heart subsided.

The cat turned away and went to the pile of rubble. She made a soft, chirruping sound. Something moved.

"What is it?" whispered Mew-sheri.

And then she saw.

Kittens!

A nest of them, curled up and warm.

She went closer. Two were gray, two black. They were the size of her hand. She longed to touch them.

The cat hovered, anxious, protective. The kittens mewed. They wanted milk, but their mother would not come to them.

"I'm making you afraid," said Mew-
sheri.

She retreated slowly, and squatted by
the doorway, keeping still. After a while
the mother cat lay down and the kittens
began to suck.

Mew-sheri watched them. She thought:
this is why she did not come to the temple.
She could not leave her kittens. She
had to wait for me to come and help her.

The cat sat up. The kittens were full
and sleepy.

Mew-sheri approached the cat.
Somehow she had to move the kittens.

"I need a basket," she said.

She remembered the wrap she had
thrown around her shoulders: a strip of
linen, big enough for a makeshift bag.
She took it off and spread it out on the
floor. The cat watched her.

Is she wild? Mew-sheri wondered. She
won't let me take them if she's a wild
desert cat.

She put out a hand and gently touched the cat's head. The cat tensed, but she did not hiss or back away as a wild cat would. Mew-sheri stroked her. Soon she felt the cat relax.

"We must move your kittens," said Mew-sheri.

Slowly she reached out, took up a sleeping kitten, and placed it on the linen. The cat watched.

The kitten opened its eyes briefly, sneezed, and slept again. Mew-sheri moved another kitten. Then another. Then the last. When they were all safe in the center of the cloth she gathered up the edges and tied them together.

The cat ran to the door, stepped outside, and began trotting back towards the village. Mew-sheri followed her.

It was only then that Mew-sheri remembered her father, and how worried he would be if he woke up and found her gone. She quickened her pace.

But when they reached the inn, Tah-hotep was still asleep. Mew-sheri put down the bundle of kittens on the floor and ran to wake him.

"Father!" she said. "I've found the Queen Cat!"

Chapter Four

By sunrise, everyone was on the roof, awake and talking: Tah-hotep, Osar, the innkeeper and his wife, and a serving girl who said she'd often given scraps to the cat.

"She's descended from the old quarry workers' cats," said the innkeeper. "She comes here for food."

"But tonight," said Mew-sheri, "she came to find me. Look at her. She is the Queen Cat."

They all gazed at the cat, and the cat gazed calmly back at them. In the daylight Mew-sheri could see her more clearly: the slim body, dark gray in color, the high pointed ears, the long face, and narrow gold eyes. Tiya had said she might not be  beautiful, and she was not, but she was queenly, assured, and Mew-sheri knew that she was the one.

41

Tah-hotep turned to Mew-sheri. He said gravely, "Neferet, I think you have found her. We must take her to the temple."

Mew-sheri smiled proudly. Her father had called her by her real name, and for the first time it seemed to fit her.

Mew-sheri, the new priestess, stood in the temple courtyard. All around her were people, but the only one she knew was her sister Tiya. She held tightly to Tiya's hand.

The cat and her kittens were not there. They had been taken away to be seen by the First Servant of the goddess. Only he could decide whether or not the cat was

truly the Queen Cat.

"What if he doesn't like her?" Mew-sheri whispered anxiously. "What if he chooses another cat? I won't be able to bear it."

"Leave it to the goddess," said Tiya. "If she is the Queen Cat they will find the secret mark of the goddess on her."

The crowd rustled. Feet and skirts moved aside and the cat ran into the center of the courtyard. There was a golden collar around her neck.

Mew-sheri looked up at Tiya. Tiya smiled. "We have a new Queen Cat," she whispered.

The crowd began to move. Mew-sheri knew that the priests would now carry the good news to the people waiting outside the temple gates. "All is well," they would say. "The goddess has returned to us."

The Queen Cat came to Mew-sheri and rubbed against her legs and purred. An old priestess then appeared, carrying a basket of kittens. She placed it in Mew-sheri's arms.

45

"Welcome to the service of the goddess," she said. "What is your name, child?"

"My name," said Mew-sheri, "is Neferet."